PENGUIN BOOKS

The Penguin Book of Private Eye Cartoons

Richard Ingrams was born in London in 1937. He was educated
at Shrewsbury and University College, Oxford. He joined
Private Eye in 1962, becoming editor the following year. He is the
author of *God's Apology* (a chronicle of three friends –
Hugh Kingsmill, Hesketh Pearson and Malcolm Muggeridge),
Goldenballs, Romney Marsh and the Royal Military Canal
and *Piper's Places: John Piper in England and Wales*. With John
Wells he has written *Mrs Wilson's Diary* (also adapted for
the stage by Joan Littlewood) and *Dear Bill: The Letters of Denis
Thatcher*. He has edited several *Private Eye* anthologies as
well as collections of Beachcomber and Cobbett. He is married
with two children and lives in Berkshire.

The Penguin Book of

PRIVATE EYE CARTOONS

Selected and Introduced by Richard Ingrams

Penguin Books

Penguin Books Ltd, Harmondsworth, Middlesex, England
Penguin Books, 40 West 23rd Street, New York, New York 10010, U.S.A.
Penguin Books Australia Ltd, Ringwood, Victoria, Australia
Penguin Books Canada Ltd, 2801 John Street, Markham, Ontario, Canada L3R 1B4
Penguin Books (N.Z.) Ltd, 182-190 Wairau Road, Auckland 10, New Zealand

These cartoons first published by *Private Eye* Productions
This selection published by Penguin Books 1983

Made and printed in Great Britain by
William Clowes and Sons Ltd, Beccles

INTRODUCTION

The cartoons in the very early *Private Eyes* were almost all the work of William Rushton. I met him first when we were both, at the age of twelve, new boys at Shrewsbury School. Willie was therefore the first cartoonist I knew and it was mainly thanks to him that I came to appreciate cartoonists and cartoons. Like many others, he was entirely self-taught and I doubt if he ever had any formal drawing lessons. Cartooning came naturally to him and he spent most of his time covering every spare corner of blank paper and even some text books with grotesque heads – mostly men in bowler hats with bulbous eyes and heavy moustaches.

To begin with there were hardly any cartoons of a conventional kind in the *Eye*. The Rushton drawings were nearly all illustrations of articles. It was two or three years before he began to do 'spot' cartoons (that is, funny drawings with or without captions). These were of an unusual variety, featuring as they did obese men and women, often in the nude. 'Hither, Gloria, I'll take a shillingsworth' was one memorable caption, as was my own favourite, the policeman apprehending two elderly homosexuals lying in bed together in the street: 'Adults you are, consenting you may well be, but I would question the privacy of Lowndes Square'.

By this stage, encouraged perhaps by the new air of licence, the *Eye* had already begun to welcome a few refugees from *Punch*. There was some reluctance at the start, and one or two were warned by *Punch* that they would not be allowed to serve two masters. I think Michael Heath was the first to try his hand and he has remained with the *Eye* ever since – surely the most prolific and consistently funny of modern cartoonists. Gradually as the years went by, a number of older hands – Anton, Leslie Starke, Scully and ffolkes – began to send in cartoons. Other more notorious converts were Gerald Scarfe and Ralph Steadman who naturally resented the way in which *Punch* editors interfered with their work ('Very good. But I think the feet should be re-drawn,' Bernard Hollowood once wrote to Scarfe).

I have not included anything by either Scarfe or Steadman in this collection as their work was almost all topical and political. Other old stagers like Trog and John Kent have been omitted for the same reason.

The cartoons are not presented in chronological sequence for the reason that some cartoonists seem to have periods of great inspiration lasting a few years, after which they fade away. If the cartoons were arranged in order, it would be seen that, at any one time in the *Eye*'s history, a particular cartoonist predominates over the others. When William Rushton absconded to become a television personality during the mid-Sixties, his successor as the most prolific contributor was Bill Tidy, another cartoonist who at that time felt inhibited by *Punch*. A devout Northerner, living in Southport, Tidy has the characteristic of many cartoonists in that he looks a bit like one of his own drawings. He and 'Larry' (Terence Parkes) began sending cartoons to the *Eye* at about the same time, and although Bill later dropped 'spot' cartoons in favour of 'strips' like the Cloggies, Larry has continued to contribute, on and off, ever since.

For me, Martin Honeysett represents the spirit of the Seventies in the *Eye*. Considerably younger than any of those so far mentioned, he was born in 1943 and studied briefly at Croydon Art School. Unlike Tidy's brash, self-confident figures, Honeysett's people all look distinctly scruffy and seedy, suggesting that everything, not only the furniture, is falling apart. Another newcomer during this period was Kevin Woodcock who specializes in architectural fantasies and surreal effects. Although he has contributed now for over ten years to the *Eye*, I have yet to meet him. I saw him once on a BBC2 *Arena* programme about *Private Eye* cartoonists. An elusive bearded Liverpudlian living in Leicester, he said he had started off life putting advertisements in the local paper offering to paint people's pets.

From the little I saw on that programme, Woodcock, working in his Leicester garret, seemed to epitomize the lonely life that many cartoonists live. Unlike other *Private Eye* contributors who think up jokes in pairs (or even threes and fours), they sit alone dependent entirely on their own inspiration for ideas. It seems an unenviable life. The rewards are not very great and there must be a constant fear that one day the well of ideas will dry up. I often marvel at the continuing inventiveness of cartoonists like Michael Heath and Edward McLachlan whose monster rabbits and hedgehogs became a regular feature in the *Eye* during the Seventies. Like Heath, McLachlan, who also lives in Leicester, seems to have a never-ending flow of ideas. Just when I think we have seen the last of him another package of his huge roughs – often nearly as detailed as the finished drawings – arrives with an apologetic note for the long delay.

How do they do it? How can they still ring the changes from what seems at first sight to be a limited number of situations? Can there be any more jokes about men coming home to find wives waiting in ambush or notes propped up on the kitchen table to say where the dinner is? It is extraordinary how they manage somehow to find variations on all such themes, as well as breaking new ground and uncovering fresh subjects. Some go in for a particular type. Hector Breeze (another hardy annual) has his tramps; Hugh Burnett his monks; John Maddocks his Arabs. The inspired John Glashan creates a strange world of his own inhabited by small bearded men permanently threatened by huge ungainly women. The more Rabelaisian Michael ffolkes explores the world of literature and even Greek myths in search of inspiration.

Even more encouraging is the way new, young cartoonists keep coming forward to take the place of their exhausted predecessors. It is always an exciting moment when in the pile of cartoons submitted, most of which are inevitably abysmal, one discerns the traces of talent in an unknown contributor, the representative of a new generation of cartoonists. Of those to emerge in the last year or so, I would mention especially Nick Newman, Alan de la Nougerede, Cluff, and Brian Bagnall, all of whom seem capable of great things.

In all the tasks I have carried out as editor of *Private Eye*, going through the cartoons, which I keep in an old cardboard box at the side of my desk, is one that has never palled over the years. When there is a lull, I dip into the box and fish out the roughs, knowing that in the fifty to a hundred drawings that come in in the course of a fortnight there will be at least three or four that will bring a smile to my lips. That, I should add, is my only criterion.

In conclusion I would just like to thank all the cartoonists who are included here for all the pleasure they have given me, and the readers of the *Eye*, during its twenty-two years of life. To them I dedicate this book.

RICHARD INGRAMS
February 1983

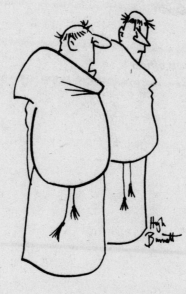

"There's talk of redundancies!"

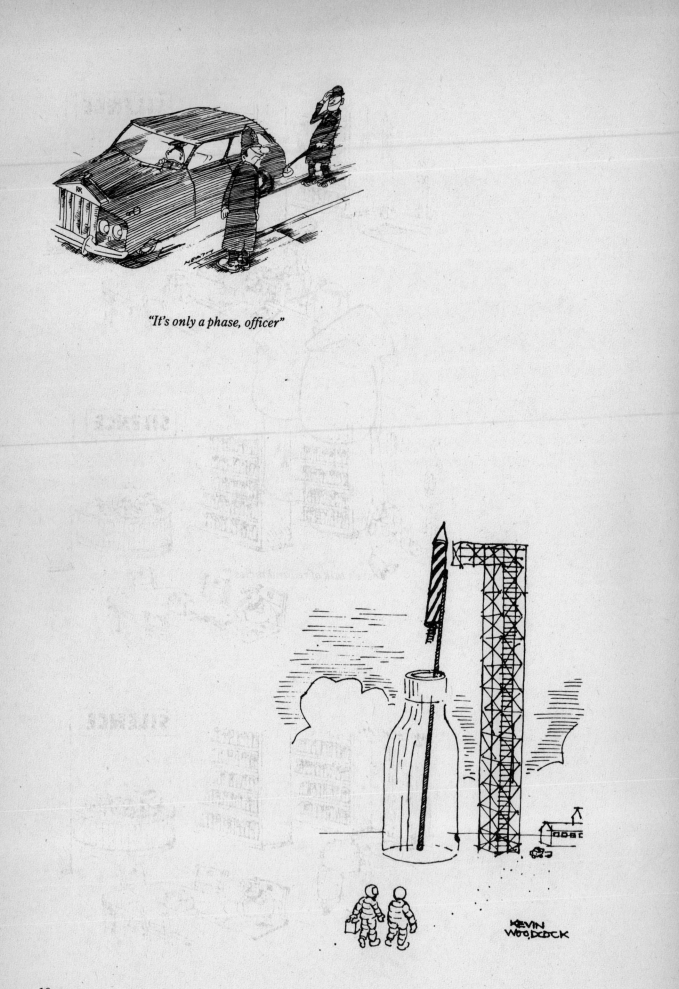

"It's only a phase, officer"

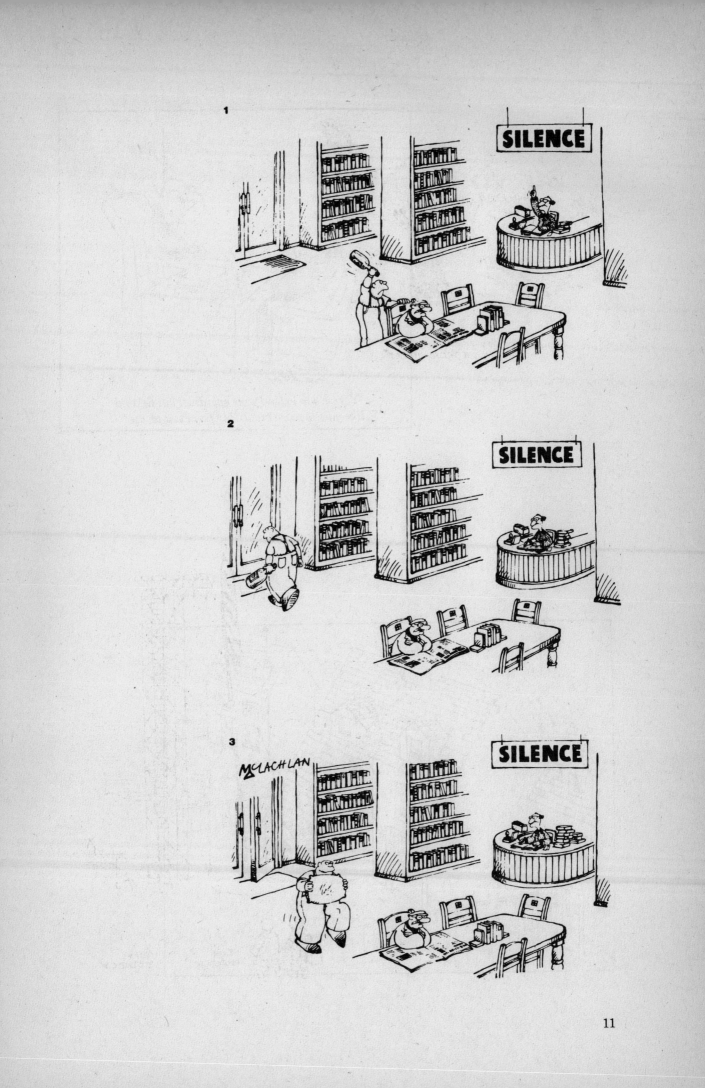

"Yes we can extend your overdraft but first I'd like a little more grovelling from you please"

"I told you never to ring me at the office!"

"Holmes, there must be some other way for you to concentrate on the Folkestone case"

16

"Arthur loves his new job with the fairground — gets a company car as well"

"The corporal here's got this great idea for a sequel!"

"Not another bloody sequel!"

"I'm an encyclopaedia salesman..."

"Poor chap thinks he's suffering from delusions . . ."

"Like a damn' fool I came out of the hole backwards but it saved my life"

"For goodness sake, why don't you take him to a hairdresser like any normal father would!?!"

"Good Lord, Fenton, I had no idea you had died!"

"It was your chairman's last wish"

"Those damned tourists are back again"

24

"Sorry, didn't we tell you? We changed it to best out of three..."

"Here they come!"

"He's at a difficult age"

27

"I'll be glad when there's just One Nation.
I never did like the other one"

30

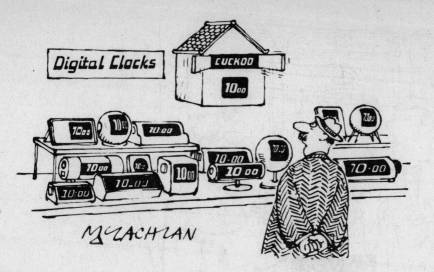

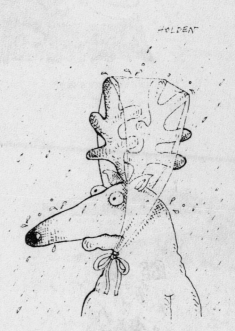

"Looks like rain, dear . . ."

31

"Er . . . mind if we swear?"

"This **surely** must be the thick end of the wedge"

"There's bound to be violence when idiots persist in carrying this kind of money around"

"What made him really ill, doctor, is worrying
about the inconvenience the visit will cause you"

"See what I mean, Sergeant? Pakistanis can't stand the smell of a bacon sandwich!"

"The new Italian sofa's attacked Daddy!"

34

"For heaven's sake, Alice, you've got to be firm with these salesmen"

"You twit! That's Everest over there!"

"Come on in, the waiter's lovely"

35

"Will you please take your feet
off my best chair!"

"I'm a 'don't know'. Don't know whether
to smash your face in or not"

"Tomorrow will be in the low seventies with scattered showers"

"I think we've found a cure for cancer"

"These are fine, I'll take these"

"I've decided to go forth and multiply – !"

38

"Tell me, dear, exactly who is this actress Connie Lingus about whom one hears so much these days?"

INTIMACY TAKING PLACE GO VIA

"Have you got anything for dirty hair, man?"

"Great news. I'm incurable!"

*"Look here, Hugget, the Committee would like to know
why you're not wearing a club moustache"*

HEATH

*"How dare you talk like that to the woman
I'm shacking up with"*

FRANK BOUGHT
HIM FROM A
SAILOR .....

..... SUCH A
QUIET BIRD AND
DO YOU KNOW,
I'VE NEVER HEARD
HIM USE A SWEAR
WORD YET.

EDWARD
McLACHLAN

"Do I hear any advance on £10,000 for this beautiful
vase, and a place in the lifeboat?"

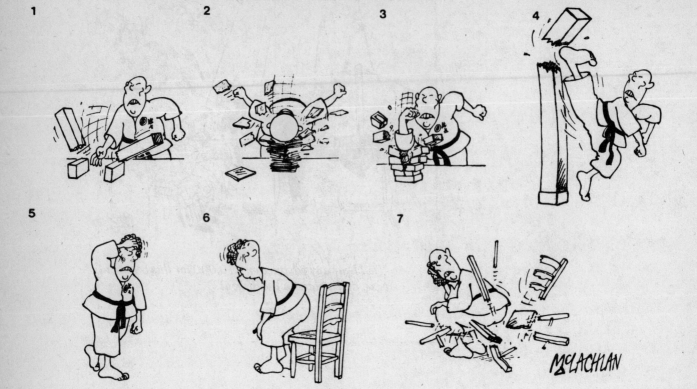

"There, just as I told you –
he's a transvestite"

47

"Who gives this women to be hit?"

"Don't be too critical of the lad, George"

"Yes! I recognize every one of them!"

51

"... and this time get it right!"

"Oh! Threatening us with karate now is he?"

GUILTY M'LUD

"You, Sir, are an impostor"

"You can turn the telly on all by yourself
now, can't you, Kevin?"

"We'll have two bottles of whatever it was they had"

55

"My God. It's Hell out there!"

"With or without lipstick?"

"Adults you are, consenting you may well be,
but I would question the privacy of Lowndes Square"

"We can do without your down to earth realism, Henshaw"

"Gad, I could do with an Eskimo woman right now!"

"Good luck, Minister – and when you lie remember to look straight into the cameras!"

"And this is my wife Media"

If only I'd had the sex education...

John Glashan

"You've been a great disappointment to your father"

"God has also chosen me to speak to you about insurance"

"Go on – beat the lights – Syd would have wanted it that way"

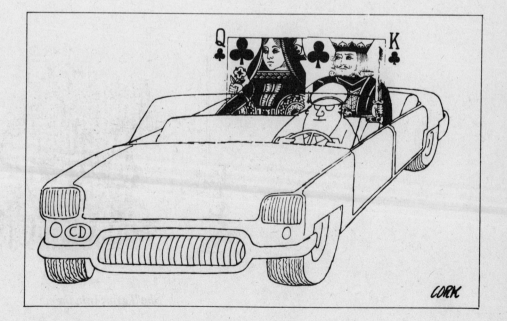

NASTY NIP
IN THE AIR,
LOBETHRUST

"She'll grow into them"

64

"Ready? They're coming"

65

"If the police start asking questions I shall just say that you packed your things one night and left me"

"I like to keep the garden looking nice and smart"

"Oh God! Not the Gay Gordons again!"

"And it grieves me to see that in spite of the education we have tried to give you your writings in the lavatories are not witty but merely coarse"

SCOTLAND YARD BAFFLED!

"Louder!!"

"Last holy orders please!"

"If one of you bastards can prove you're his natural son, you'll get the lot . . ."

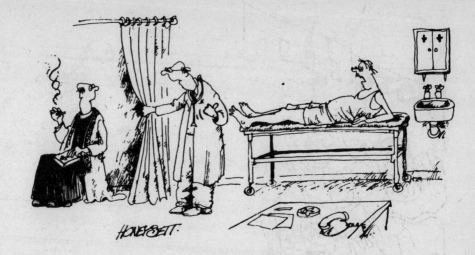

"Tell me doc, how bad is it?"

"You'll like this, sir. It'll make you both very drunk"

WAY OUT

KEVIN WOODCOCK

BUN BANK

BANK

BANK

this is a COCK-UP

DEPOSITS

Raymonde

"From now on I'm keeping a low profile"

72

"You'll have to shout, he's a bit deaf"

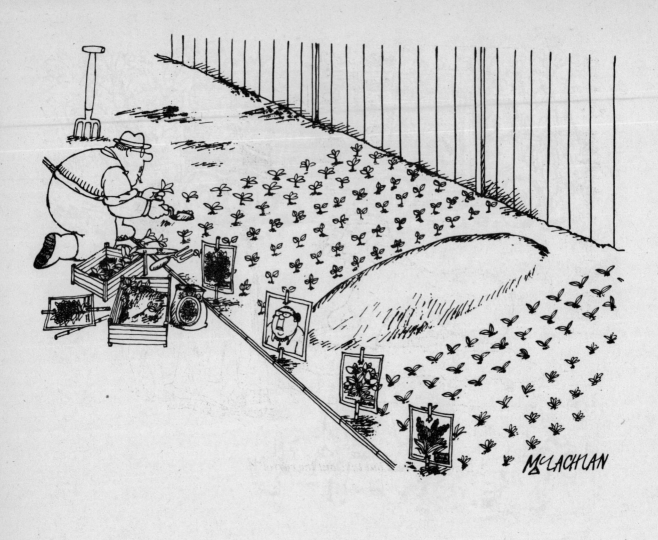

74

"Basically I like it but take out the carrot"

"You bastard!"

"Mrs Grimshaw? Here's your ʃⁱᶜᵏᵘʳ ᵐᵗⁱᵍˢᵘₛ"

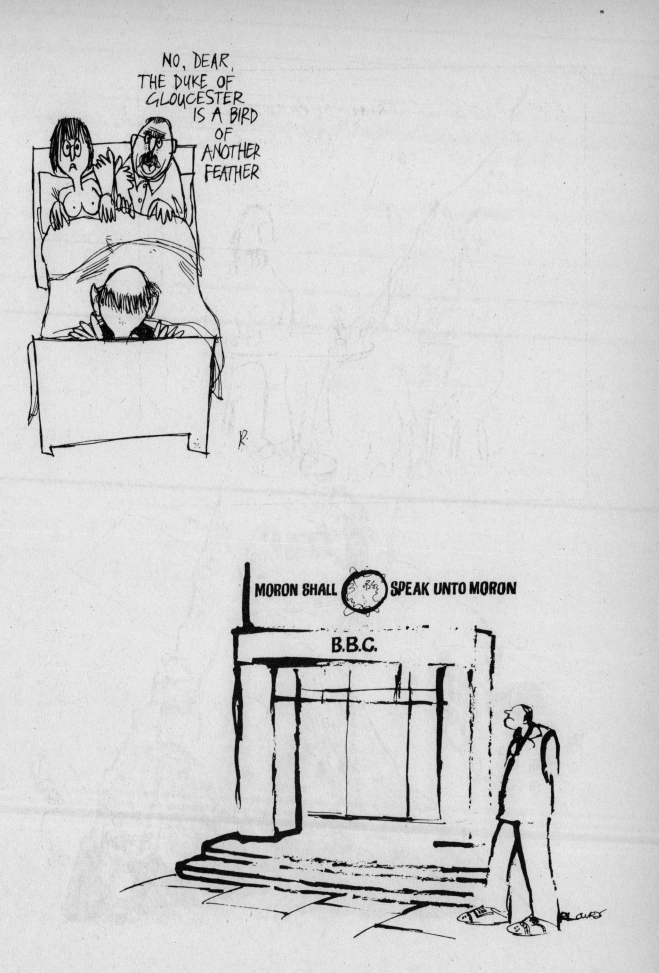

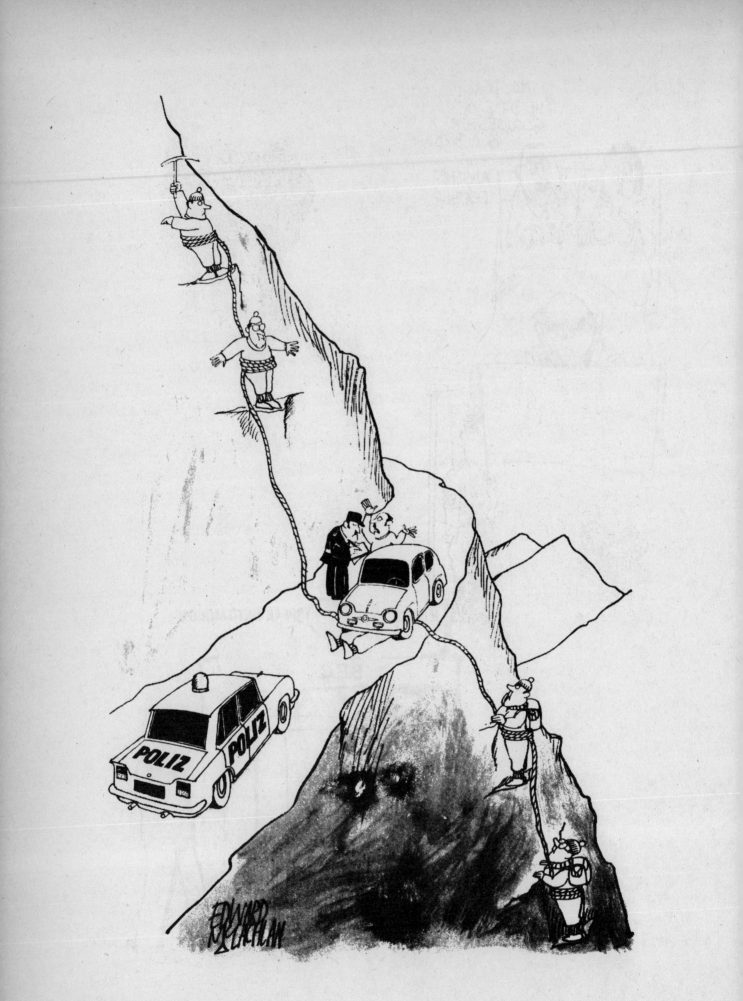

"I'd learn a trade son, . . . this isn't
going to last forever . . ."

"Why don't you ever dress up
as Albert Schweitzer?"

It's been PREYING on
my mind for some
weeks now, that
you might be
enjoying yourself ...

John Glashan

McLACHLAN

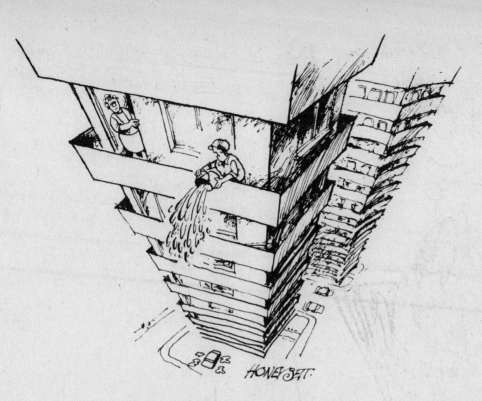

"Hang on, I'll just finish washing the car"

I think working class people are marvellous —

Yes, I love the sharp animal-like way their eyes dart about ...

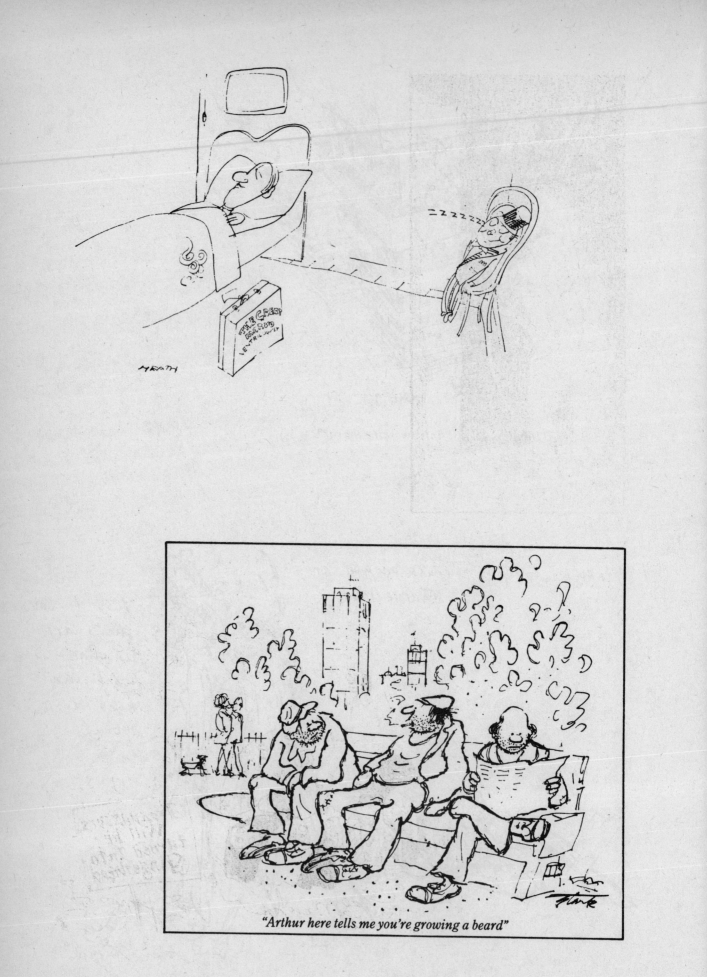

"Arthur here tells me you're growing a beard"

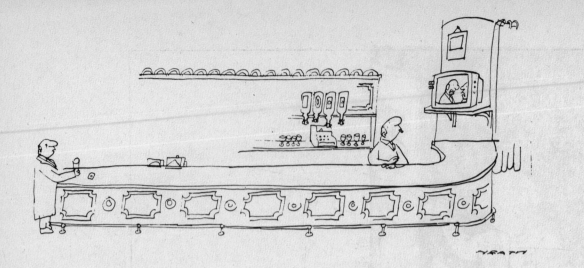

"When the commercials come on could I have half of bitter?"

"I now declare these swimming baths open"

84

"Any obsolescent material?"

"My God – They've found out!"

McLACHLAN

"Do you think a contraceptive pill might cheer her up a bit?"

"Gentlemen, gentlemen! Disorder, please, disorder!"

"I've been looking for that everywhere"

"Well what did we expect Tarzan to look like after all these years?"

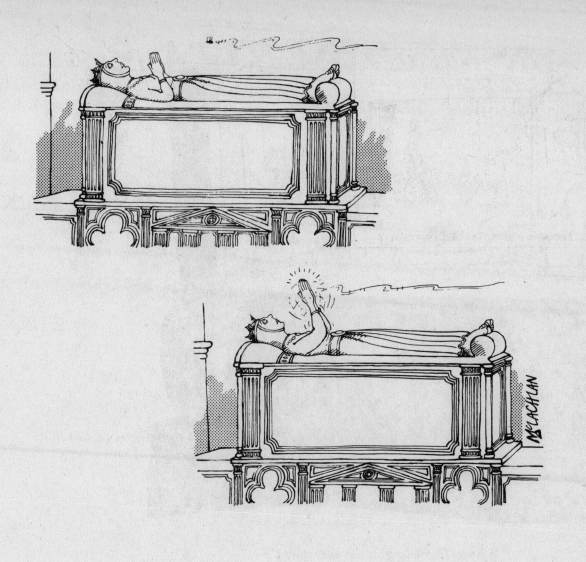

"Rameses the Second was a bloody wog! Not British!"

"Oh dear! I wonder if it's our baby sitter?"

KEVIN WOODCOCK

"Considering he's only just changed sex, it's not a bad effort"

90

"Don't worry, there'll be another one along in a minute"

". . . and if you look to your right you will see that we have just knocked somebody over"

"In the beginning . . .'
Are you listening, Hilda?"

"I see 'Thou shalt not commit adultery''s
dropped to eighth . . ."

"Are you Pop or Dada?"

"When I was a boy we had to make our own entertainment"

"Oh no! Not that old cliché again"

96

"Another poison pen letter!"

"I'm all for cleaning up television, Miss Whitby, but let's keep life filthy!"

*"That's what the ploughman has for lunch,
fish fingers and chips"*

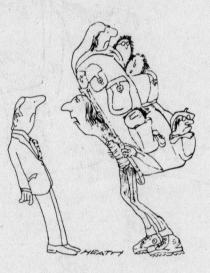

"I've got squatters"

"Couldn't you read the paper in the morning like other husbands?"

"It's the chance of a lifetime, Bellingham. Buckingham Palace is one of the plum jobs!"

"STOP! Stop this debauchery!"

"You're taking a chance, aren't you?"

S. GROSS

*"My wife! Say I'm busy – in conference – tell her **anything**"*

"He's on the couch with Miss Burnham"

"Go on boy, rabbits, go get 'em!"

"Does anybody know whether they're supposed to do that?"

"I wish you'd use the nutcrackers, dear"

"It's a digital sun-dial, dear"

"It was . . . AAAAAAAGGGGGGGHHHHH . . ."

"George Herbert AAAAAAAGGGGGGGGHHHHH? We have reason to believe . . ."

"I don't think it was intended for quadruplets"

"Sexism!"

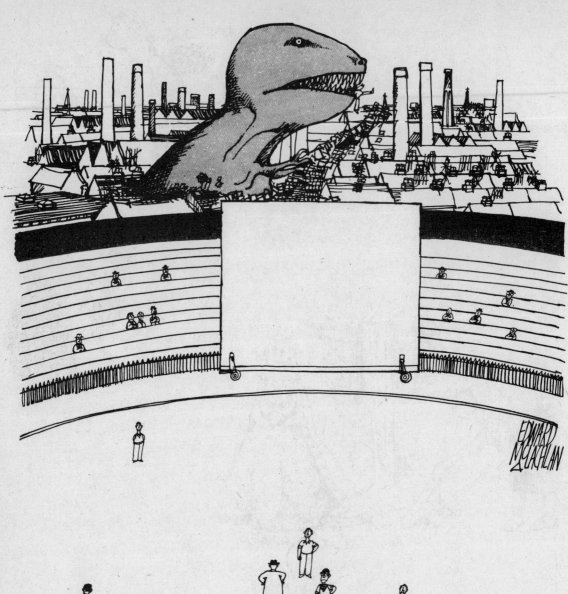

"...And once again we have interruption of play
caused by movement behind the bowler's arm..."

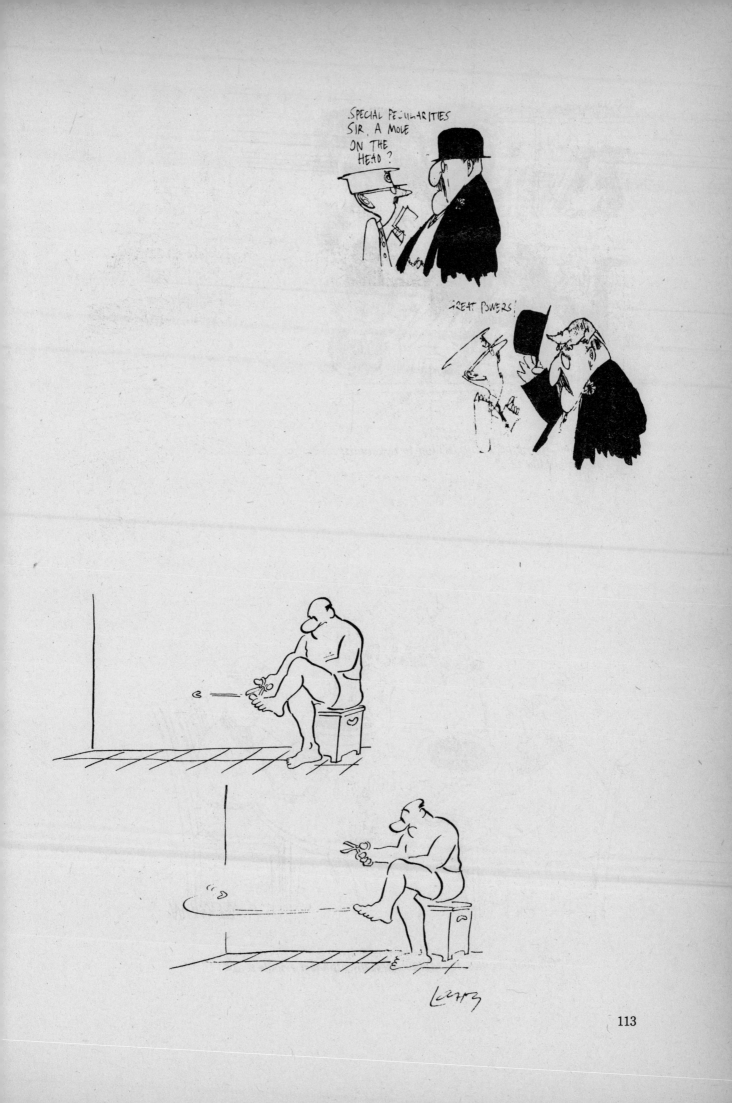

113

"By God, Hornpipe, I wouldn't like to be a nudist on a night like this"

"Oh, look, mother, it's Mabel's special – alphabet noodle soup"

"And if you fixed the roof you wouldn't have to stay in every time it rained"

"Does this damned thing have a reverse?"

116

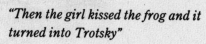

"Then the girl kissed the frog and it turned into Trotsky"

"We had sex today"

"This is his answering service"

"Anything to get out for a pint"

THESE DAYS A POPULAR
CROP ROTATION IS, BARLEY
TURNIPS, POP FESTIVAL,
WHEAT . . . .

AGRICULTURAL COLLEGE

"Of course, ideally, it should be a tiger's skin"

"Great Heavens! A Roaring Poof!"

123

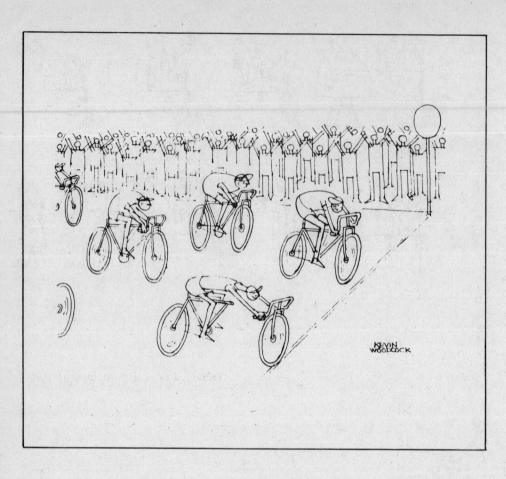

"*Improve yourself somewhere else, son – we're all equal here!*"

"Have you any crisp-flavoured crisps?"

"I'm terribly worried I might live!"

"... and it's well beyond the range of Cable TV".

"Sorry to drag you out like this, Doctor"

"Dumbkopf."

"Going to go mad this year?"

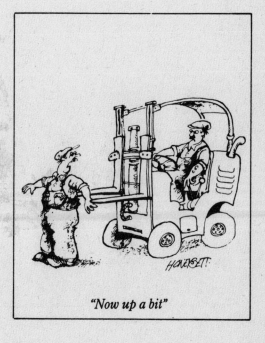

"Now up a bit"

"Watch out Glenda, here come some of those awful gypsies"

"Don't rush, Nellie! Poise!"

"And remember to call in for a vasectomy on your way home"

"We call her Melody. She lingers on"

"You're not having any more sweets until you go and put your teeth in"

"Well, we can't have a holiday there again – you've been sentenced to death in your absence"

133

"Room service? I don't seem to have a Gideon's bible"

"Er . . . plus VAT, sir"

134

"It's a fully automatic camera, it even goes to Boots on its own"

"My husband is very particular about his food"

"Never mind, Mrs Brown. Release your marker buoy"

136

"Read the bit again where I disinherit the whole family"

"You must find it a terrible strain being funny day after day"

"I'm sorry, vicar – I accidentally activated my anti-rape alarm . . ."

"Sorry to trouble you but this gentleman thinks he
left some chewing gum under that seat"

"Of course you're depressed. I'm very expensive"

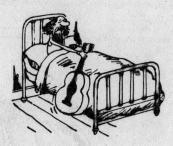

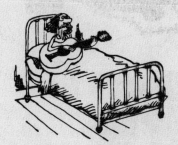

*"Aye, strange
things can
happen at sea"*

145

"I don't want comforting. I want a cure for boils"

*"Stay! The night is young
and you are enormous"*

*"Forget the sunshine league,
where's Brightsea in the
sewage league?"*

"It's his old steam radio"

"It's from Jane. She's living in sin with someone called Tarzan!"

148

*"It's the most sophisticated camera in the world,
but I can't find anything worth photographing"*

"Don't colour the whole thing red, Purdy. Just sizeable chunks"

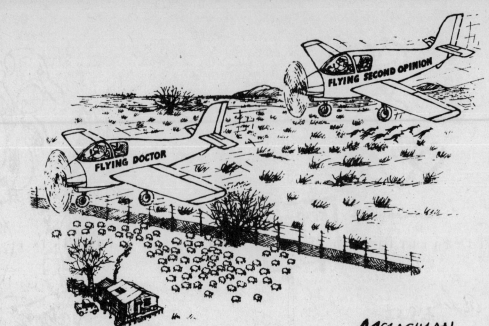

McLACHLAN

"I presume you're aware that Eskimo Nell has had
rather a chequered past . . .?"

"How do you like your stake?"

"This could mean war! Archduke Franz should be carrying the spare wheel!"

". . . and a little man from the village delivers our vegetables"

"It's mince again!"

"I granted his death wish"

"Sorry about the shortage of glasses . . ."

"Stop looking guilty, Benson!"

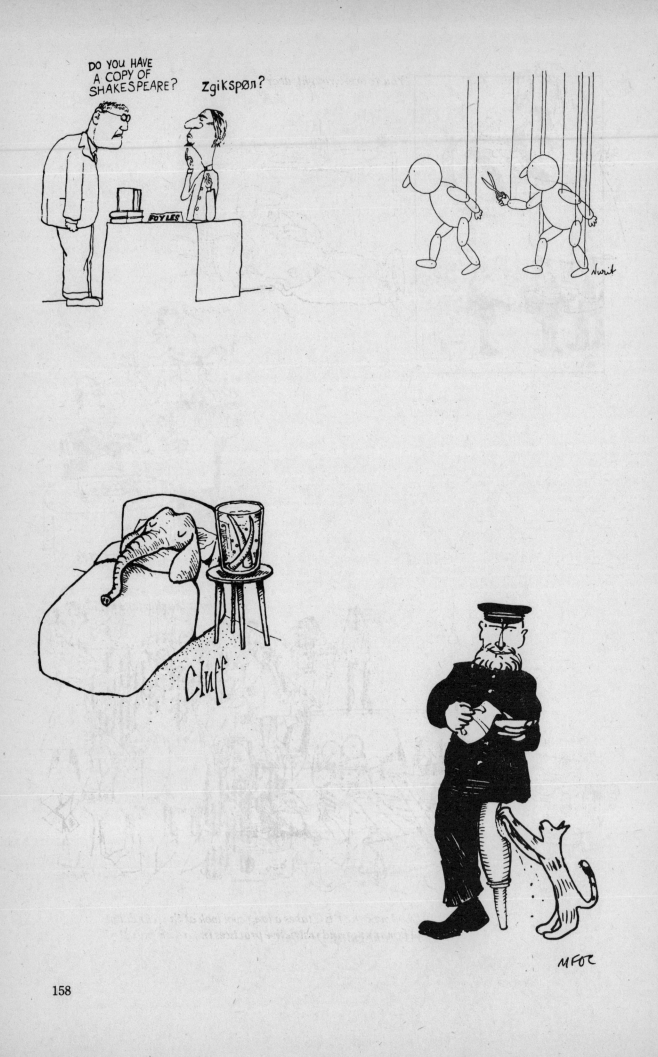

"You're overwrought, dear"

"And now the BBC takes a long cool look at the scandal of overmanning and restrictive practices in British Industry"

"Well, you did say they should go outside and get some fresh air"

"Well, we haven't made a very good start have we, Mrs Turnstone?"

"Take your seats for the last supper"

"Turn left where it says 'Lesbians Unite', right when you get to 'Gay Boys Rule'..."

McLACHLAN

"I'll have to hang up, Dora. I've got a real kink here"

"And I say you're going around with the wrong set!"

"For God's sake Harry, let go of the elephant"

"You're a very dirty old monk!"

"*Bugger off – I'm considering
the lilies of the field!*"

169

KEVIN WOODCOCK

McLACHLAN

"Take a card, any card"

"What I like about this place is that it's completely unspoiled"

"All my books are best sellers, but this unfortunately doesn't prevent me from being a very boring person to meet"

"Clockwise, Knucklehead!"

*"Chong Ding Foo! Ha ha! you asked for **cat food!**"*

"Beach overcrowded again"

"These are extremely realistic, Madam.
After a week the petals fall off"

"You've done it now, David. Here comes his mother!"

"Well Trenshaw, this is the last chance for our super-intelligence drug XLR6. I've just given the rat the injection"

"Yet another one dead!! That's it, I guess . . . it doesn't work. Take it away!"

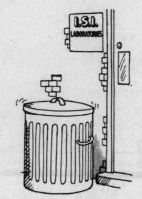

"I see Benson's overcome his fear of flying"

"*Then for twenty years he was on Aircraft Carriers*"

"Who taught your kettle to swear like that?"

Congratulations,
Mrs. Ravensmoor,
you've got a
dead husband ...

John Glashan

McLACHLAN

Bitter?   No. Just tired.

"— and here we are again in Trafalgar Square..."

INDEX

Entries indicate the pages on which cartoons appear in this book. *Private Eye* issue numbers and dates of publication also appear.

47 Cork, 546, *19.11.82*
   Anton, 221, *20.6.70*
   Rushton, 123, *2.9.66*

48 Kevin Woodcock, 452, *13.4.79*
   De La Nougerede, 508, *5.6.81*

49 Kevin Woodcock, 411, *16.9.77*
   Honeysett, 312, *30.11.73*

50 McLachlan, 227, *28.8.70*

51 Nick Baker, 461, *17.8.79*
   Bill Tidy, 97, *3.9.65*
   Maddocks, 487, *15.8.80*

52 ffolkes, 487, *15.8.80*
   Bill Tidy, 102, *12.11.65*
   Austin, 387, *15.10.76*

53 Glynn Boyd Harte, 126, *14.10.66*
   Maddocks, 457, *22.6.79*
   W. Scully, 231, *23.10.70*

54 McLachlan, 390, *26.11.76*
   Larry, 184, *3.1.69*

55 Rushton, 32, *8.3.63*
   Heath, 387, *15.10.76*
   Nick Baker, 390, *26.11.76*

56 ffolkes, 478, *11.4.80*
   Honeysett, 387, *15.10.76*

57 Rushton, 118, *24.6.66*
   S. Gross, 118, *24.6.66*

58 Honeysett, 394, *21.1.77*
   Bill Tidy, 103, *26.11.65*

59 Hugh Burnett, 244, *23.4.71*
   Heath, 274, *16.6.72*

60 Honeysett, 299, *1.6.73*
   Larry, 302, *13.7.73*
   Starke, 323, *3.5.74*

61 John Glashan, 323, *3.5.74*
   Heath, 126, *14.10.66*

62 Calman, 97, *3.9.65*
   Honeysett, 302, *13.7.73*
   Larry, 155, *24.11.67*
   Croft, 300, *15.6.73*

63 Larry, 493, *7.11.80*
   Cork, 491, *10.10.80*

64 Rushton, 26, *14.12.62*
   Heath, 498, *16.1.81*
   Honeysett, 290, *26.1.73*

65 John Glashan, 334, *4.10.74*
   Honeysett, 306, *7.9.73*

66 Bill Tidy, 297, *4.5.73*
   Honeysett, 297, *4.5.73*
   Larrry, 209, *19.12.69*

67 McLachlan, 302, *13.7.73*
   Ken Pyne, 463, *14.9.79*

68 Honeysett, 299, *1.6.73*
   Larry, 323, *3.5.74*

69 Sillince, 86, *1.4.65*
   Bill Tidy, 110, *4.3.66*

70 Austin, 462, *31.8.79*
   Hector Breeze, 89, *14.5.65*
   Bill Tidy, 86, *1.4.65*

71 Honeysett, 323, *3.5.74*
   Baker, 308, *5.10.73*
   Rushton, 92, *25.6.65*

72 Raymonde, 20, *21.9.62*
   Kevin Woodcock, 309, *19.10.73*
   Heath, 463, *14.9.79*

73 McLachlan, 393, *7.1.77*
   Honeysett, 352, *13.6.75*
   Austin, 390, *26.11.76*

74 McLachlan, 331, *23.8.74*
   Kevin Woodcock, 545, *5.11.82*

75 ffolkes, 308, *5.10.73*
   Heath, 434, *4.8.78*
   Brian Bagnall, 553, *25.2.83*

76 Glashan, 331, *23.8.74*
   Glashan, 96, *20.8.65*

77 Rushton, 96, *20.8.65*
   R. Lowry, 301, *29.6.73*

78 McLachlan, 218, *24.4.70*

79 Bill Tidy, 93, *9.7.65*
   Hector Breeze, 87, *16.4.65*
   Bill Tidy, 107, *21.1.66*

80 Glashan, 329, *26.7.74*
   McLachlan, 389, *12.11.76*

81 Honeysett, 325, *31.5.74*
   Glashan, 372, *19.3.76*

82 Heath, 384, *3.9.76*
   Starke, 324, *17.5.74*

83 Austin, 392, *24.12.76*
   ffolkes, 447, *2.2.79*

84 Heath, 369, *2.6.76*
   Honeysett, 322, *19.4.74*

85 Heath, 321, *5.5.74*
   Hugh Burnett, 137, *17.3.67*

86 McLachlan, 440, *27.10.78*
   Bill Tidy, 98, *17.9.65*

87 Fantoni, 310, *2.11.73*
   Rushton, 97, *3.9.65*
   Larry, 195, *6.6.69*

88 Honeysett, 286, *1.12.72*
   Heath, 309, *19.10.73*
   Kevin Woodcock, 429, *26.5.78*

89 McLachlan, 397, *43.3.77*
   Bill Tidy, 89, *14.5.65*

90 W. Scully, 298, *18.5.73*
   Kevin Woodcock, 308, *5.10.73*

91 Rushton, 80, *8.1.65*
   McLachlan, 395, *4.2.77*

92 Mike Williams, 398, *18.3.77*
   Heath, 407, *22.7.77*

93 Hector Breeze, 310, *2.11.73*
   Bill Tidy, 81, *22.1.65*
   Rushton, 101, *29.10.65*

94 S. Gross, 286, *1.2.72*
   Hector Breeze, 464, *28.9.79*

95 Honeysett, 307, *21.9.73*
   W. Scully, 276, *14.7.72*

96 Adamson, 303, *27.7.73*
   Kevin Woodcock, 486, *1.8.80*

97 McLachlan, 263, *14.1.72*
   Bill Tidy, 108, *4.2.66*

98 Heath, 307, *21.9.73*
   Heath, 438, *29.9.78*
   Rushton, 70, *21.8.64*

99 Mike Williams, 135, *17.2.67*
   Kevin Woodcock, 401, *29.4.77*

100 Bill Tidy, 116, *27.5.66*
    Bill Tidy, 78, *11.12.64*
    Bill Tidy, 112, *1.4.66*

101 Bill Tidy, 404, *10.6.77*
    S. Gross, 117, *10.6.66*

102 McLachlan, 488, *29.8.80*
    Bill Tidy, 135, *17.2.67*

103 McLachlan, 134, *3.2.67*
    Kevin Woodcock, 487, *15.8.80*

104 Zimego, 129, *25.11.66*
    Rushton, 122, *19.8.66*
    Kevin Woodcock, 396, *18.2.77*

105 McLachlan, 351, *30.5.75*

106 Lowry, 353, *27.6.75*
    Honeysett, 305, *24.8.73*

107 McLachlan, 498, *16.1.81*
    Honeysett, 467, *9.11.79*

108 Honeysett, 357, *22.8.75*
    McLachlan, 462, *31.8.79*

109 Kevin Woodcock, 482, *6.6.80*
    McLachlan, 340, *10.1.75*

110 ffolkes, 481, *23.5.80*
    McLachlan, 519, *6.11.81*

111 Heath, 419, *6.1.78*
    Honeysett, 304, *10.8.73*
    Starke, 298, *18.5.73*

112 McLachlan, 234, *4.12.70*

113 Rushton, 38, *31.5.63*
    Larry, 196, *20.6.69*

114 Rushton, 106, *7.1.66*
    McLachlan, 276, *14.7.72*

115 Larry, 196, *20.6.69*
    Honeysett, 316, *25.1.74*

116 Starke, 294, *23.3.73*
    ffolkes, 293, *9.3.73*

117 Maddocks, 473, *1.2.80*
    Larry, 292, *23.2.73*

118 Heath, 298, *18.5.73*
    Hector Breeze, 56, *7.2.64*
    Larry, 274, *16.6.72*

119 Starke, 274, *16.6.72*
    Kevin Woodcock, 433, *21.7.78*

120 Kevin Woodcock, 472, *18.1.80*
    ffolkes, 275, *30.6.72*

121 Honeysett, 293, *9.3.73*
    Honeysett, 298, *18.5.73*
    Larry, 62, *1.5.64*

122 Heath, 295, *6.4.73*
    Colin Wheeler, 266, *25.2.72*
    Honeysett, 291, *9.2.73*

123 Starke, 290, *26.1.73*
    Heath, 275, *30.6.72*

124 Kevin Woodcock, 460, *3.8.79*
    Maddocks, 449, *2.3.79*

125 Heath, 362, *31.10.75*
    Hugh Burnett, 379, *25.6.76*
    Nick Baker, 545, *5.11.82*

126 Honeysett, 399, *1.4.77*
    ffolkes, 361, *17.10.75*

127 *McLachlan, 293, 9.3.73*
Colin Wheeler, 227, 28.8.70
Honeysett, 291, 9.2.73
128 *Heath, 271, 5.5.72*
Maddocks, 438, 29.9.78
S. Gross, 407, 22.7.77
129 *Hector Breeze, 180, 8.11.68*
Fantoni, 273, 2.6.72
Rushton, 50, 15.11.63
130 *Bill Tidy, 188, 28.2.69*
Hector Breeze, 274, 16.6.72
Kevin Woodcock, 461, 17.8.79
131 *McLachlan, 461, 17.8.79*
Maddocks, 448, 16.2.79
132 *ffolkes, 442, 24.11.78*
Honeysett, 442, 24.11.78
133 *S. Gross, 276, 14.7.72*
Larry, 180, 8.11.68
Hector Breeze, 278, 11.8.72
134 *Kevin Woodcock, 363, 14.11.75*
Brian Bagnall, 556, 8.4.83
Heath, 463, 14.9.79
135 *Fantoni, 287, 15.12.72*
Heath, 260, 3.12.71
Kevin Woodcock, 443, 8.12.78
136 *Kevin Woodcock, 467, 9.11.79*
Thomson, 545, 5.11.82
Bill Tidy, 160, 2.2.68
137 *Larry, 85, 19.3.65*
Ken Pyne, 421, 3.2.78
138 *ffolkes, 259, 19.11.71*
De La Nougerede, 558, 6.5.83
Larry, 272, 19.5.72
139 *Heath, 418, 23.12.77*
Rushton, 32, 8.3.63
Kevin Woodcock, 409, 5.8.77
140 *Honeysett, 306, 7.9.73*
Kirby, 500, 13.2.81
141 *Rushton, 65, 12.6.64*
ffolkes, 404, 10.6.77
142 *Kevin Woodcock, 405, 24.6.77*
Cork, 363, 14.11.75
Starke, 260, 3.12.71
143 *McLachlan, 378, 11.6.76*
144 *Maddocks, 444, 22.12.78*
ffolkes, 270, 21.4.72
145 *McLachlan, 182, 6.12.68*
McLachlan, 161, 16.2.68
Bill Tidy, 159, 19.1.68
146 *Kevin Woodcock, 441, 10.11.78*
ffolkes, 454, 11.5.79
147 *Kevin Woodcock, 439, 13.10.78*
Bill Tidy, 161, 16.2.68
Heath, 227, 28.8.70
148 *Fantoni, 235, 18.12.70*
Honeysett, 438, 29.9.78
Bill Tidy, 186, 13.1.69
149 *Kevin Woodcock, 420, 20.1.78*
Heath, 545, 5.11.82
150 *Cluff, 557, 24.4.83*
Newman, 557, 24.4.83
ffolkes, 457, 22.6.79

151 *Adamson, 465, 12.10.79*
Heath, 317, 8.2.74
Kevin Woodcock, 319, 8.3.74
Austin, 359, 19.9.75
152 *McLachlan, 437, 15.9.78*
Bill Tidy, 108, 4.2.66
153 *S. Gross, 150, 15.9.67*
Colin Wheeler, 237, 15.1.71
McLachlan, 431, 23.6.78
154 *Honeysett, 421, 3.2.78*
Kevin Woodcock, 428, 12.5.78
155 *Bill Tidy, 208, 5.12.69*
Fantoni, 263, 14.1.72
156 *Ross, 437, 15.9.78*
ffolkes, 252, 13.8.71
157 *Cork, 351, 11.7.75*
Maddocks, 468, 23.11.79
Heath, 368, 23.1.76
158 *Fantoni, 203, 26.9.69*
Nurit, 466, 26.10.79
Cluff, 555, 25.3.83
M. O'Connor, 489, 12.9.80
159 *Heath, 264, 28.1.72*
Rushton, 161, 16.2.68
160 *Arnold Wiles, 316, 25.1.74*
Honeysett, 421, 3.2.78
161 *McLachlan, 423, 3.3.78*
Rushton, 12, 1.6.62
162 *Heath, 422, 17.2.78*
McLachlan, 365, 12.12.75
163 *Honeysett, 371, 5.3.76*
Bill Tidy, 112, 1.4.66
164 *McLachlan, 295, 6.4.73*
165 *Bill Tidy, 110, 4.3.66*
Winn, 558, 6.5.83
Heath, 461, 17.8.79
166 *Honeysett, 302, 13.7.73*
Cork, 491, 10.10.80
167 *Rushton, 34, 5.4.63*
Hugh Burnett, 145, 7.7.67
Kevin Woodcock, 457, 22.6.79
168 *Honeysett, 370, 20.2.76*
Maddocks, 486, 1.8.80
169 *Larry, 194, 23.5.69*
Cork, 429, 26.5.78
Hugh Burnett, 141, 12.5.67
170 *Kevin Woodcock, 499, 30.1.81*
Heath, 358, 5.9.75
McLachlan, 466, 26.10.79
171 *McLachlan, 355, 25.7.75*
Honeysett, 362, 31.10.75
172 *Cork, 351, 11.7.75*
Larry, 349, 2.5.75
173 *Heath, 360, 3.10.75*
Heath, 336, 1.11.74
174 *Cork, 490, 26.9.80*
Raymonde, 487, 15.8.80
175 *Bill Tidy, 156, 8.12.67*
Adamson, 436, 1.9.78
Cork, 474, 15.2.80

176 *ffolkes, 483, 20.6.80*
Honeysett, 460, 3.8.79
177 *McLachlan, 471, 4.1.80*
Kevin Woodcock, 492, 24.10.80
178 *Heath, 145, 7.7.67*
Kevin Woodcock, 461, 17.8.79
179 *McLachlan, 335, 18.10.74*
180 *Heath, 465, 12.10.79*
Larry, 484, 4.7.80
181 *Raymonde, 464, 28.9.79*
Honeysett, 451, 30.3.79
182 *Maddocks, 466, 26.10.79*
Larry, 157, 22.12.67
Kevin Woodcock, 548, 17.12.82
183 *Heath, 274, 16.6.72*
Larry, 376, 14.5.76
184 *John Glashan, 370, 20.2.76*
McLachlan, 357, 22.8.75
185 *John Glashan, 98, 17.9.65*
Maddocks, 467, 9.11.79
S. Gross, 135, 17.2.67
186 *Kevin Woodcock, 305, 24.8.73*